WELCOME TO PASSPORT TO READING

A beginning reader's ticket to a brand-new world!

Every book in this program is designed to build read-along and read-alone skills, level by level, through engaging and enriching stories. As the reader turns each page, he or she will become more confident with new vocabulary, sight words, and comprehension.

These PASSPORT TO READING levels will help you choose the perfect book for every reader.

READING TOGETHER
Read short words in simple sentence structures together to begin a reader's journey.

READING OUT LOUD
Encourage developing readers to sound out words in more complex stories with simple vocabulary.

READING INDEPENDENTLY
Newly independent readers gain confidence reading more complex sentences with higher word counts.

READY TO READ MORE
Readers prepare for chapter books with fewer illustrations and longer paragraphs.

This book features sight words from the educator-supported Dolch Sight Words List. This encourages the reader to recognize commonly used vocabulary words, increasing reading speed and fluency.

For more information, please visit passporttoreadingbooks.com.

Enjoy the journey!

Little, Brown and Company

Hachette Book Group
1290 Avenue of the Americas, New York, NY 10104
Visit us at lb-kids.com

Little, Brown and Company is a division of Hachette Book Group, Inc.
The Little, Brown name and logo are trademarks of Hachette Book Group, Inc.

The publisher is not responsible for websites (or their content)
that are not owned by the publisher.

First Edition: October 2015

Library of Congress Control Number: 2015941633

ISBN 978-0-316-37727-0

10 9 8 7 6 5 4 3 2

CW

Printed in the United States of America

Passport to Reading titles are leveled by independent reviewers applying the standards developed by Irene Fountas and Gay Su Pinnell in *Matching Books to Readers: Using Leveled Books in Guided Reading*, Heinemann, 1999.

Adapted by Jennifer Fox

Based on the episode "Boys vs. Girls"

written by John Loy

LITTLE, BROWN AND COMPANY

New York Boston

Attention, Teen Titans fans!
Look for these words when you read
this book. Can you spot them all?

car

cheetah

truck

cootie catcher

VRRRRM! VRRRRM! VRRRRM!
Beast Boy zooms around
on a crazy car.

BURP!

Cyborg lets out

a huge stinky burp.

"We are being such boys!"
Robin says.

"BOYS! BOYS! BOYS!"
they shout.

“Quiet!” Raven yells.

“What is her problem?”
Cyborg asks.

“Girls have cooties!”
Robin says.
“Boys are better than girls.”

"Prove it," Raven says.

It is time for a contest.
It is boys versus girls.

First, Beast Boy
and Starfire race.

"It is cheetah time,"
Beast Boy says.
Starfire flies by
him so fast.

Next, Robin and Raven
must solve a math problem.
"You are going down,"
Robin says.

Raven is very smart
and finishes fast.
"Done!" she shouts
just as Robin starts.

Last, the teams
have a tug-of-war.

Cyborg transforms
into a turbo truck
to make him strong.

It is a close contest.

Raven's magic makes the girls stronger than the boys!

BOYS 0

GIRLS 3

The girls win!
Cyborg and Beast Boy
join the girls team.

"GIRLS! GIRLS! GIRLS!"
they shout.

Robin still wants to prove boys are better than girls. He has a plan.

He sneaks into a lab
and steals some cooties.

That night,
Robin slips cooties
into the girls' rooms.

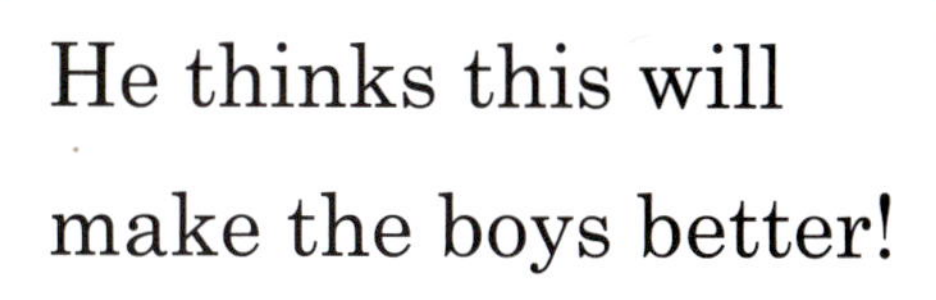
He thinks this will
make the boys better!

The next day,
Raven and Starfire
feel itchy.

"My skin is crawling,"
Raven says.

“Cooties!” the boys yell.

The girls have an idea.
They will catch the boys
and give them cooties, too.

"Run!" Robin shouts.

JUMP
CITY

The girls are fast.
They catch the boys.
“Now we all have
cooties,” Starfire says.

Robin uses the cootie catcher!

The team is cured!

The boys and girls agree that the best thing is being cootie-free.